The Gingerbread Man

Retold by
Hugh Lupton

Illustrated by
Diana Mayo

Barefoot Books
Celebrating Art and Story

Once there lived a boy called Ollie Blaster, and one day he went to visit his two aunts, Aunty Hetty and Aunty Betty. They decided to make a gingerbread man, so they mixed:

eggs

flour

sugar

milk

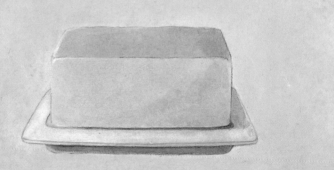

butter

and ginger.

They rolled it with a rolling pin and cut it into shape.
They gave it currant eyes and a cherry mouth.

When it was ready for the oven, Ollie Blaster looked it up
and down. "I think I'll call you Johnny Cake," he said.

Very, very carefully they lifted Johnny Cake onto a baking tray. Very, very carefully they put the baking tray into the oven and closed the oven door. Then Aunty Hetty and Aunty Betty said, "Ollie, we're going outside to do some gardening. You stay inside and watch the oven."

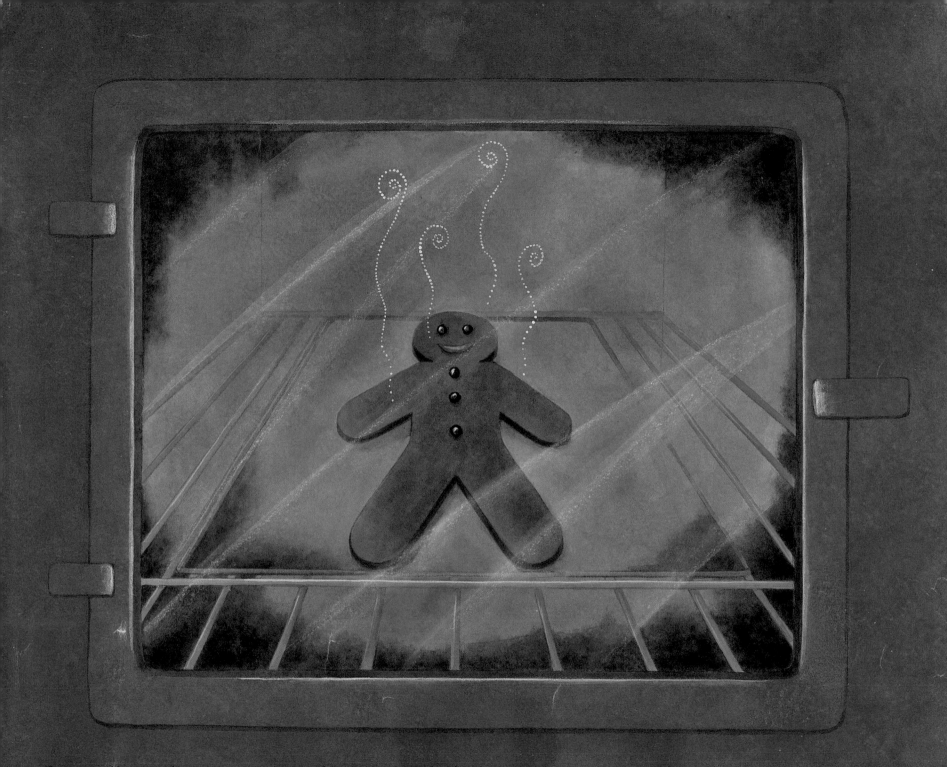

So Ollie Blaster sat and watched the oven. He watched it for a very long time ... and his eyes were just closing, his head was just nodding, he was just about to fall asleep, when a strange thing happened.

Suddenly, the oven door burst open ... and out jumped Johnny Cake! He was steaming golden-brown and he smelled delicious.

BANG!

He gave a
little bow and said,
**I can run faster
than you!**
And then he turned on his
heel and he was away
across the kitchen floor.

Ollie Blaster leapt to his feet. "Oh no, you can't!" he said, and he set off running after him ...

and he ran and he ran,
but soon he was left far behind.

Well, Johnny Cake ran out of the kitchen, down the steps and through the garden … and there were Aunty Hetty and Aunty Betty digging potatoes. Johnny Cake threw back his head and shouted:

I can run faster than Ollie Blaster,

And I can run faster than you!

And Aunty Hetty and Aunty Betty said, "Oh no, you can't!" And they dropped their forks and they lifted up their skirts and they set off after Johnny Cake ... and they ran and they ran, but soon they were left far behind.

Well, Johnny Cake ran through the garden gate and along the street … and there were two men digging a ditch. Johnny Cake threw back his head and shouted:

I can run faster than Ollie Blaster,

I can run faster than Hetty and Betty,

And I can run faster than you!

And the two Ditchers said, "Oh no, you can't!"
And they leapt out of the ditch and set off after Johnny Cake ...
and they ran and they ran, but soon they were left far behind.

Well, Johnny Cake ran along the street and around a bend … and there were two old women, sitting in the sunshine, stitching and sewing. Johnny Cake threw back his head and shouted:

I can run faster than Ollie Blaster,   I can run faster than Hetty and Betty,

I can run faster
than Ditchers,

And I can run
faster than you!

And the two Stitchers said, "Oh no, you can't!" And they dropped
their stitching and sewing and they set off after Johnny Cake ...
and they ran and they ran, but soon they were left far behind.

Well, Johnny Cake ran under a fence and into a wood ...
and there were Bear and Hare, sharing a piece of sweet, yellow
honeycomb. Johnny Cake threw back his head and shouted:

I can run
faster than
Ollie Blaster,

I can run
faster than
Hetty and Betty,

I can run
faster than
Ditchers

and Stitchers,

And I can run faster than you!

And Bear and Hare said, "Oh no, you can't!"
And they dropped the honeycomb and set off
after Johnny Cake ... and they ran and they
ran, but soon they were left far behind.

Well, Johnny Cake ran out of the wood and along a hedge ...
and there was Mr. Fox, sitting preening his whiskers.
Johnny Cake threw back his head and shouted:

I can run
faster than
Ollie Blaster,

I can run
faster than
Hetty and Betty,

I can run
faster than
Ditchers

| and Stitchers, | I can run faster than Bear and Hare, | And I can run faster than you! |

And Mr. Fox pricked up one ear and said, "I'm sorry, I'm just a little bit deaf. I can't quite hear what you're saying. I wonder if you could come just a little bit closer, and I wonder if you could speak just a little bit louder?"

Well, Johnny Cake stopped running then; he took one … two …
three … steps closer to Mr. Fox. And now he was standing with
his steaming golden-brown tummy pressed against Mr. Fox's wet
nose, and Mr. Fox could smell the delicious gingerbread smell
and his mouth was watering. Johnny Cake took a deep breath,
and he said at the top of his voice:

I can run faster than Ollie Blaster,
I can run faster than Hetty and Betty,
I can run faster than Ditchers and Stitchers,
I can run faster than Bear and Hare,

And I can run faster than you!

And, do you know, those were the last words that he ever spoke.
Mr. Fox opened his mouth and ...

SNAP! MUNCH! CRUNCH!

He gobbled up Johnny Cake, licked his lips, wiped his mouth
with the back of his paw and sloped away through the bushes.
And that was the end of Johnny Cake.
And that's the end of the story.

For Cosmo and Joseph – H. L.
For Mum and Dad, with love – D. M.

Barefoot Books
3 Bow Street
Cambridge, MA 02138

This book was typeset in Bembo Schoolbook
The illustrations were prepared in acrylics on hotpress watercolor paper

Graphic design by Louise Millar, London
Color separation by Grafiscan, Italy
Printed and bound in China by South China Printing Co. Ltd

This book has been printed on 100% acid-free paper

Library of Congress Cataloging-in-Publication Data

Lupton, Hugh.
    The gingerbread man / retold by Hugh Lupton ; illustrated by Diana Mayo.—1st ed.
[24] p. : col. ill. ;   cm.
Summary: A freshly baked gingerbread man escapes when he
is taken out of the oven and eludes a number of hungry animals
until he meets a clever fox.
ISBN 1-84148-056-8
1. Fairy tales. 2. Folklore. I. Mayo, Diana. II. Title.
398.21 E 21   2003

1 3 5 7 9 8 6 4 2

Make your own gingerbread!

Ingredients
8 tbsp butter
1/2 cup caster sugar
1 cup flour
1 egg
2 teaspoons ground ginger
Pinch of salt
Cup of milk

Utensils
Baking tray
Large mixing bowl
Pastry brush
Rolling pin
Wooden spoon or fork
knife

To make your gingerbread man follow these simple steps:

1. Preheat the oven to 180C / 350 F (gas mark 5).

2. Put the sugar, pinch of salt, and butter into a large bowl and mix together with a wooden spoon or fork until smooth.

3. Keep mixing while you add the egg and the ground ginger.

4. Gradually add the flour and keep mixing until there is no flour left in the bowl and you have a ball of firm dough.

5. Turn the dough out onto a flat, floured surface and roll until it is approx 1cm thick.

6. Using a knife, carefully cut out the shape of your gingerbread man. Cut out as many gingerbread men as you can until you run out of dough.

7. Add currants for eyes and a slither of cherry for the mouth.

8. Gently brush the surface of your gingerbread men with a little milk, using the pastry brush.

9. Place the dough shapes on a greased baking tray, making sure they are well spaced out.

10. Place the tray on the second shelf of the preheated oven.

11. Cook for 15 to 20 minutes, until firm to the touch and golden brown. Leave to cool and then eat!

Growing Readers
New Hanover County Public Library
201 Chestnut Street
Wilmington, NC 28401